TIP TAP
WENT THE CRAB

FOR A.P.

With thanks to Emily Ford and Kayt Manson.

First published 2010 by Macmillan Children's Books
This edition published 2012 by Macmillan Children's Books
a division of Macmillan Publishers Limited
20 New Wharf Road, London N1 9RR
Basingstoke and Oxford
Associated companies throughout the world
www.panmacmillan.com

ISBN: 978-0-230-76995-3

Text and illustrations copyright © Tim Hopgood 2010
Moral rights asserted

1 3 5 7 9 8 6 4 2

A CIP catalogue record for this book is available from the British Library.

Printed in China

Crabs have 10 legs –
8 back legs and 2 more at the front
that have grasping claws, called pincers
OUCH!

TIP TAP
WENT THE CRAB

tim hopgood

MACMILLAN CHILDREN'S BOOKS

Once there was a crab who lived under a stone in a little rock pool.

The pool was beautiful. It was full of colourful shells, strange-looking plants and tiny sea creatures.

But the little crab had grown tired of her rock pool. The big blue sea is the place for me, she thought. So off she went for a sideways walk.

Tip-tap went the crab,

past **one** noisy seagull standing on a rock.

1

Tip-tap went the crab,

past **two** sleepy sea lions dozing in the sun.

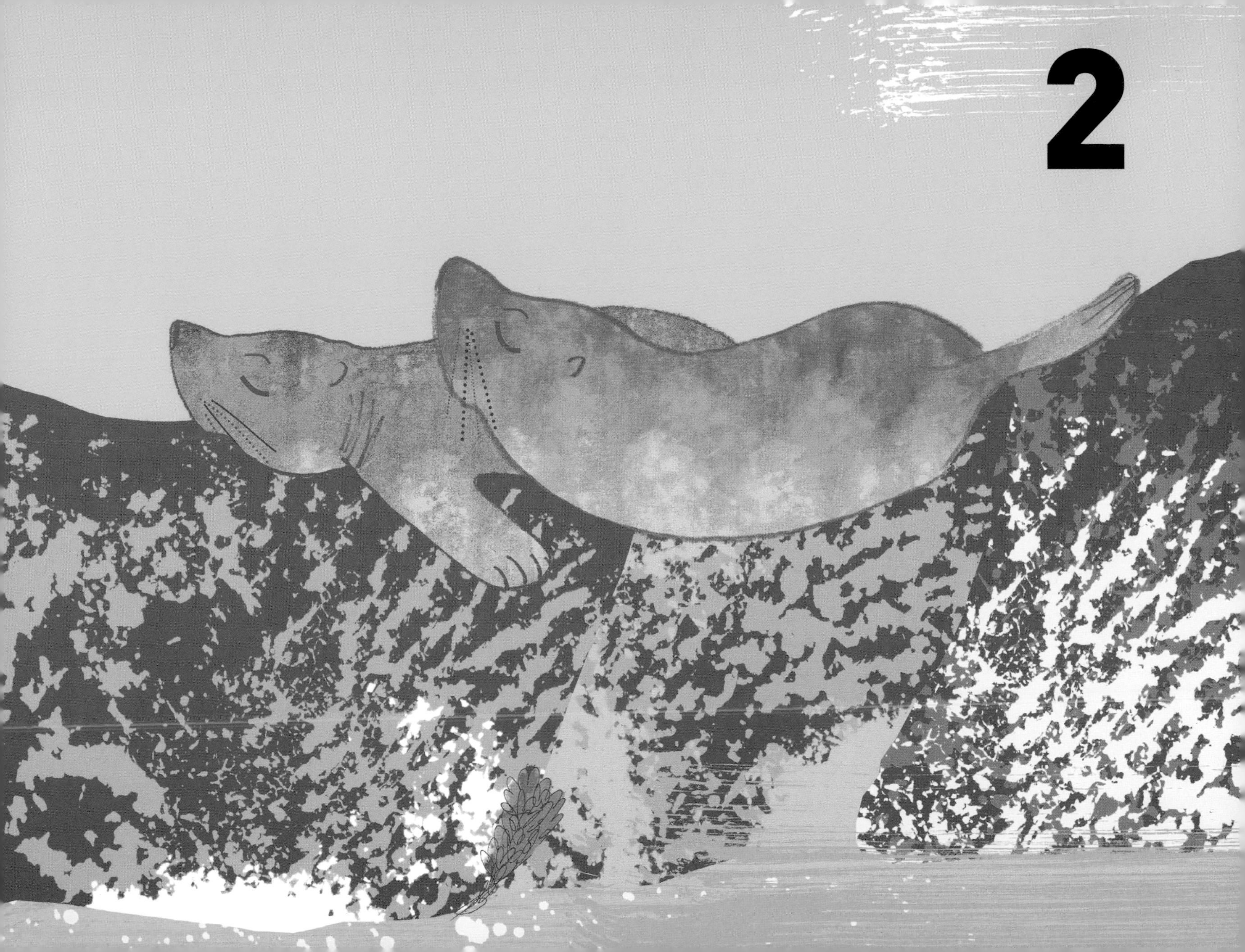
2

Tip-tap went the crab,
past **three** pointy starfish washed up
on the shore.

3

Tip-tap splash! went the crab, sideways into the big blue sea.

The little crab stopped
to look all around.

4

She saw **four** funny octopuses wriggling in the water.

5

And **five** dancing jellyfish
that bobbed up and down.

6

Tip-tap went the crab,

past **six** swimming turtles
that paddled round and round.

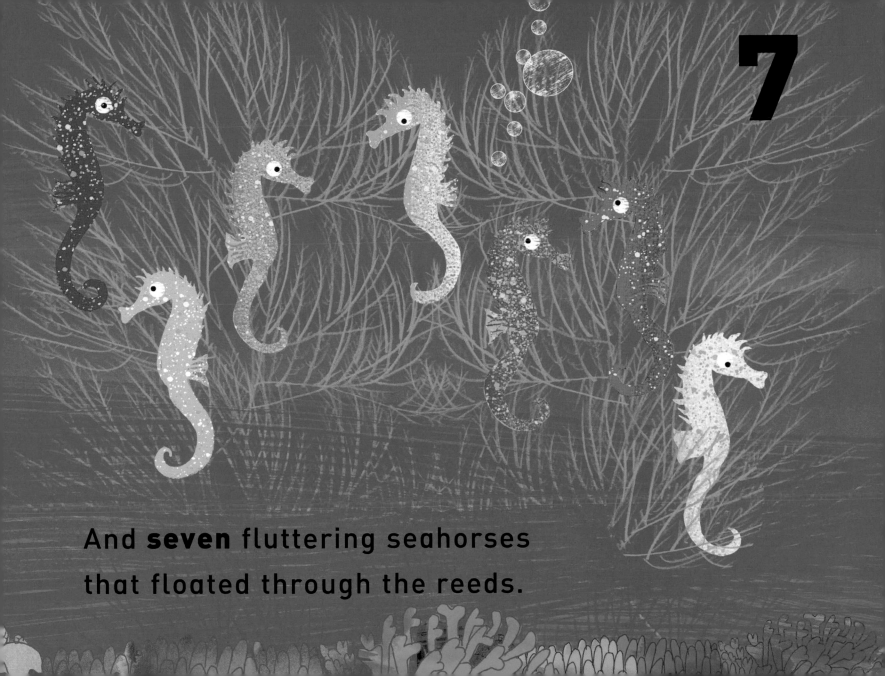

And **seven** fluttering seahorses
that floated through the reeds.

7

8

The little crab
watched as a
shoal of **eight** fish
swished left
and then right.

The big blue sea
is wonderful,
she thought.
There's so
much to see!

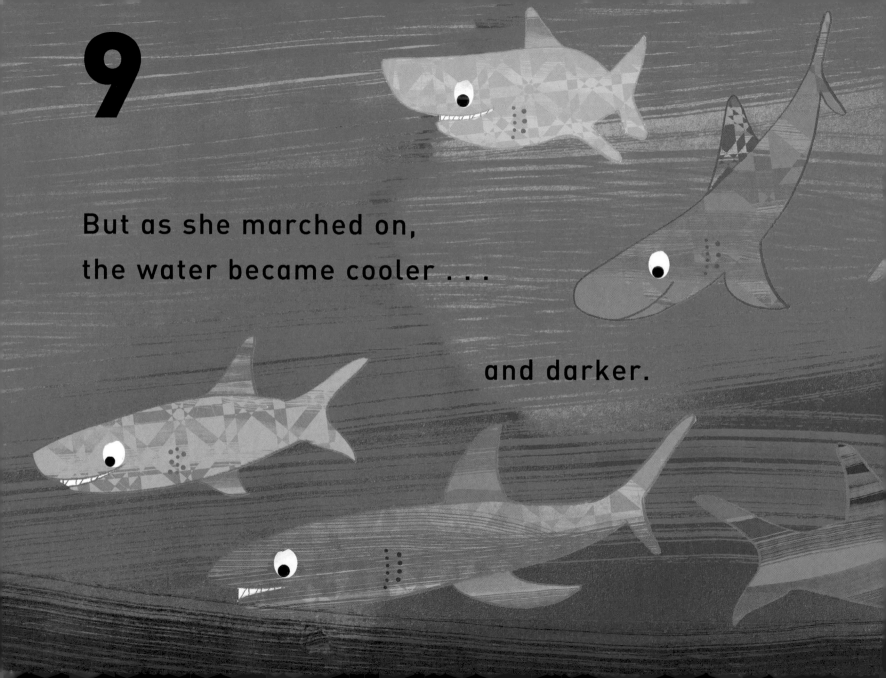

9

But as she marched on,
the water became cooler . . .

and darker.

Tip-tap, tip-tap went the crab, as quietly as she could, past **nine** silent sharks at the bottom of the sea.

At last she came to a
tip-tap stop!
This is it, thought the
crab, the perfect spot.

But after a while, she began
to miss her little rock pool.
She missed the colourful shells,
strange-looking plants and tiny
sea creatures.

The big blue sea isn't for me,
thought the little crab.

It was time to

tip-tap home.

But this time she was followed by **ten** tiny crabs.

And they all walked sideways,
just like their mum!

Tip-tap, tip-tap, tip-tippety-tap.

1 one 2 two 3 three 4 four 5 five

There are ten gold coins hidden in this pool.

Look carefully and see if you can spot them.

6 six

7 seven

8 eight

9 nine

10 ten